PRAISE FOR
Strange Weather in Tokyo

"Simply and earnestly told, this is a profound exploration of human connection and the ways love can be found in surprising new places." —*BuzzFeed*

"A moving, funny, and immersive tale of modern Japan and old-fashioned romance . . . A quiet, understated beauty of a book."
—*Book Riot*

"In quiet, nature-infused prose that stresses both characters' solitude, Kawakami subtly captures the cyclic patterns of loneliness while weighing the definition of love." —*Booklist*

"In its love of the physical, sensual details of living, its emotional directness, and above all in the passion for food, this is somewhat reminiscent of Banana Yoshimoto's *Kitchen*."
—*Independent* (UK)

"Each chapter of the book is like a haiku, incorporating seasonal references to the moon, mushroom picking and cherry blossoms. The chapters are whimsical and often melancholy, but humor is never far away . . . It is a celebration of friendship, the ordinary and individuality and a rumination on intimacy, love and loneliness. I cannot recommend *Strange Weather in Tokyo* enough, which is also a testament to the translator who has skillfully retained the poetry and beauty of the original." —Japan Society

"*Strange Weather in Tokyo* is a tender love story that drifts with the lightness of a leaf on a stream. Subtle and touching, this is a novel about loneliness, assuaged by an unlikely romance, and brought to life by one of Japan's most engaging contemporary writers."
—*Readings* (Australia)

"A dreamlike spell of a novel, full of humor, sadness, warmth, and tremendous subtlety. I read this in one sitting, and I think it will haunt me for a long time."

—AMY SACKVILLE, author of
Painter to the King and *The Still Point*

PRAISE FOR
Manazuru

"In Kawakami's first novel to be translated into English, a woman fades in and out of the present as she visits the beach town of Manazuru, in the shadow of Mt. Fuji. The real and the fantastical meld as Kei narrowly avoids disaster (she escapes the typhoon that destroys the restaurant where she was dining). Her memories are startlingly vivid, yet their veracity remains uncertain; are the visions she has of her husband with another woman real or imagined? Kawakami has a remarkable ability to obscure reality, fantasy, and memory, making the desire for love feel hauntingly real." —*Publishers Weekly*

"The action convincingly moves in waves between Kei's past and present, the surreal and the everyday. Part ghost story, part meditation on life and death, family and self, this slim novel is captivating and suspenseful, and sure to satisfy not only fans of ghost fiction but all readers." —*Booklist*

PRAISE FOR
The Nakano Thrift Shop

"Kawakami lavishes attention on quotidian minutiae and exquisitely awkward pauses, ending scenes on maddeningly unresolved but vibrant images . . . It feels a lot like daily life in Tokyo, but odder." —*The New York Times*

PARADE

PARADE

A FOLKTALE

Hiromi Kawakami

TRANSLATED FROM THE JAPANESE BY

ALLISON MARKIN POWELL

ILLUSTRATED BY

TAKAKO YOSHITOMI

Soft Skull ✺ *New York*

First published in Japan in 2002 by Heibonsha Co. Ltd.
Copyright © 2002 by Hiromi Kawakami
Illustrations copyright © 2002 by Takako Yoshitomi
Translation copyright © 2019 by Allison Markin Powell
All rights reserved

First Soft Skull edition: 2019

Library of Congress Cataloging-in-Publication Data
Names: Kawakami, Hiromi, 1958– author. | Powell, Allison Markin,
    translator.
Title: Parade / Hiromi Kawakami ; translated from the Japanese by
    Allison Markin Powell.
Other titles: Parēdo. English
Description: First Soft Skull edition. | New York : Soft Skull, 2019. |
    Originally published in Japanese by Heibonsha in 2002.
Identifiers: LCCN 2019008880 | ISBN 9781593765804 (pbk.)
Subjects: LCSH: Children—Japan—Fiction. | Tengu—Fiction. |
    Tales—Japan.
Classification: LCC PL855.A859 P3713 2019 | DDC
    895.6/36—dc23
LC record available at https://lccn.loc.gov/2019008880

Cover design & art direction by salu.io
Book design by Wah-Ming Chang
Illustrations by Takako Yoshitomi

Published by Soft Skull Press
1140 Broadway, Suite 704
New York, NY 10001
www.softskull.com

Soft Skull titles are distributed to the trade by Publishers Group West
Phone: 866-400-5351

Printed in Canada
10 9 8 7 6 5 4 3 2 1

PARADE

"TELL ME A STORY FROM LONG AGO," Sensei said.

"When you say 'long ago,' how long ago do you mean?"

"Long ago means long ago."

"I see."

Sensei and I were preparing somen noodles. I put the freshly boiled noodles in a colander and muttered, Hot, as I brought my fingertips to my earlobe.

"Does that really work, Tsukiko, touching your earlobe like that?" Sensei asked while he cut a thin fried egg into strips.

"I just assumed so, ever since seeing actresses on television shows do it."

Now that he mentioned it, though, touching my earlobe seemed like a strange thing to do when I could just as easily run my fingers under cold water. Sensei quickly finished cutting up the egg, and then set about the myoga ginger.

"Don't you think a woman touching her earlobe is a charming gesture—kind of sexy?"

"Tsukiko, that sort of thing doesn't suit you."

"Pardon me."

As I rinsed the somen, my gaze was fixed on Sensei's hands wielding the kitchen knife. Egg, myoga ginger, shiso, scallions, shredded cucumber, crushed sesame seeds, umeboshi paste, simmered eggplant. He prepared the condiments, one after another. He served each on its own small plate. I dumped the drained noodles into a large bowl, and Sensei furrowed his brow.

"Tsukiko, that simply won't do for the somen," Sensei said as he returned the noodles to the colander. He immersed the colander

7

in water again, and then he drained smaller clumps of noodles, one at a time. He wound each clump into its own bundle as he put them back in the large bowl.

"This makes it easy to pick up with chopsticks, doesn't it? Here, Tsukiko, you try it."

What difference does it make, since you're going to eat them anyway? I held back these words as I fumbled at scooping the somen noodles into separate lumps. Sensei carried the plates of condiments into the tatami room where the low table was set up. The glass doors had been flung open, and the cicadas were buzzing outside. It was Saturday afternoon.

We had eaten lunch here another time, just before the end of the rainy season. That day we'd had soba. I'd been sprawled at the low table while Sensei prepared the meal. At first he'd said, Make yourself comfortable, Tsukiko, but after a while he'd scolded me. At least you can set up the tray stand. While Sensei was swiftly coming and going between the kitchen and the tatami room, I had wiped down the table and dillydallied about, slowly bringing out some small plates. Eventually he had said to me, "You'd better just sit back down, Tsukiko. Otherwise, you'll only be in my way."

That was two weeks ago. The rainy season had ended, and the hot weather had arrived. It was true what they said about the first ten days after the rainy season always being hot and dry.

"Sensei, you're actually quite the chef, aren't you?" I said to him.

He'd once told me that he hardly ever cooked.

"Well, nowadays I have started cooking occasionally," he replied. "When my wife first ran off, I had no choice but to cook all my own meals."

"I see."

"Let's dig in, Tsukiko, shall we?"

The yellow of the egg and the green of the shiso, the lapis of the eggplant along with the pale red of the myoga ginger. Sensei and I slurped our somen noodles as we listened to the drone of the cicadas and the leaves of the cherry trees rustling in the garden. When we had eaten all of the somen that was in the bowl, Sensei went to the kitchen and emptied the rest of the noodles from the colander into the bowl and brought it back out.

"Sensei, the somen doesn't seem easier to eat this way. Haven't you just dumped all the noodles into the bowl?" When I pointed this out, Sensei looked at me with a deadpan expression. "Well, that's just the way it goes." He scattered a heap of myoga ginger into his dipping sauce and then took some noodles with his chopsticks. The songs of the min-min cicadas and the abura cicadas seemed to be vying with each other. Every so often a faint breeze would pass through, cool against the sweaty napes of our necks. We ate up the somen, devouring every last noodle.

"A full stomach makes you sleepy," Sensei said to me as I poured barley tea into his glass. I was indeed sleepy. I was going to comment on how lively the cicadas were, but I found it hard to open my mouth to speak. I realized that Sensei was lying down.

"You should have a nap too, Tsukiko," Sensei recommended drowsily.

"I couldn't do that," I replied, but Sensei sounded as though he was already half asleep. By the time his breathing had become quite regular, I found that I too had lain down. The cicadas sure are lively. This time I managed to get the words out, but now that Sensei had fallen asleep there was no one to hear me. The cicadas are lively. I murmured this to myself once more, and closed my eyes. For a while, I was still awake, but sooner or later I must have dozed off. Even within my slumber, the persistent drone of the cicadas resonated faintly in my ears.

IT FELT AS THOUGH I HAD BEEN ASLEEP FOR a long time, but about thirty minutes later I found myself awake. When my eyes opened, they met Sensei's gaze on the other side of the low table.

"You're awake," Sensei said languidly.

"I fell asleep."

"I did too, so it's okay."

"Is it really?" What, exactly, was okay? Sensei and I remained where we were, lying down. A torpor lingered within my body.

"The weave of the tatami is imprinted on my arm," I said.

"Where? Show me," Sensei said, and he stretched out his arm under the low table. I leaned mine up against Sensei's, and he propped himself up on his elbow to examine it, seeming to duck his head under the table to do so.

"Well, look at that. The tatami print is quite clearly marked on your skin."

"Isn't it?"

"On a much younger person, the marks would quickly disappear, but not on you, Tsukiko."

"That's a rude thing to say."

Sensei continued to stare at my arm, all the way down to my palm. His eyes on my palm, he murmured something about me not having any wit lines, even though I had several affair lines. The vertical lines that stick out above your heart line are your wit lines, and your affair lines are the ones that run parallel to your life line, along the base of your thumb. Look, I have many wit lines, he said.

"Tsukiko, tell me a story from long ago," Sensei said as he tapped on my palm. Sensei's hand was warm. I remembered the feeling from when I was young, of always wanting to hold someone's hand. But I did not feel the urge to hold Sensei's hand. I did not want to feel his warm hand against my own. Sensei was still tapping my palm. It was the same kind of tapping that one might do while singing a lullaby. A certain warmth spread through me from the spot where he was tapping.

"I wasn't alive long ago, but I should tell you a story from when I was little?" I said in a drawl.

Please do, Sensei replied, and slowly I began talking about things from that time, things that had risen up from deep within my body as Sensei had tapped on my palm.

I was awakened by a clamor.

The source of the noise was inside the room. It was red. Something dark red and something pale red were arguing with each other.

As I pretended to still be sleeping in my futon on the floor, I strained my ears to discern the clamor being raised by these two people. (Or were they animals?) I couldn't understand a word they were saying. Perhaps because I had just woken up and was still in a bit of a daze—just as we are now—or perhaps I was surprised by the fact that these two red people (or animals?) were in my room.

While I was listening to the clamor, my head gradually began to clear. The two beings looked exactly like the spirit creatures I had seen in folktale books—they had human bodies, red faces with long noses, and wings. You mean *tengu*? Sensei asked. Yes, these were tengu, I replied. Their faces were beautiful shades of red, just as depicted in books.

I CHANGED OUT OF MY PAJAMAS AND WENT to the kitchen, and these two followed after me. They continued to argue the whole time. Their voices were loud, and they were speaking fast. *Mother won't be pleased about this*, I thought to myself. A mother will always find fault with whatever items a child brings back into the house. Colored tiles found on the street. Scarab beetles. Tadpoles scooped out of the rice paddy. Coix seeds. Stray cats. Get rid of that, mine would say at first. I'll take care of it if you let me keep it, I would say. I won't make a mess, I would promise. Better not, my mother would reply. And my insistent entreaties would ultimately be granted.

I wondered if the tengu were things (people?) I had brought home from outside. I had no memory of doing so, but maybe they had attached themselves to me without my realizing it. But where might that have happened?

As I sat down and started to spread margarine on a piece of bread, the two of them pointed at the margarine and grew increasingly boisterous. They were extremely disruptive. My heart was pounding, waiting for my mother to lose her temper. But there she was right in front of me, perfectly calm as she held the string of her tea bag, swaying it back and forth in her cup. My mother liked to say that swaying the tea bag brought out the prettiest color in the black tea.

"Tsukiko, the tengu want to lick the margarine," my mother said. As if this were perfectly ordinary.

"Mom, aren't you surprised?" I asked, and she shook her head. She picked up the plate of margarine and handed it to the tengu, who unfurled their long tongues and began lapping away. I myself had at one time furtively licked the margarine, but I remember it immediately made me feel sick. The tengu, however, seemed unbothered. They licked up quite a good deal of the margarine.

When I put on my backpack, the tengu ran their hands all over the sturdy leather schoolbag.

"They're touching it," I said to my mother, and she laughed.

"They must think it's unusual."

Both of the tengu nodded at my mother. She nodded back at them. I found it kind of annoying, how well my mother seemed to be getting along with the tengu. After all, it was *my* room they'd shown up in.

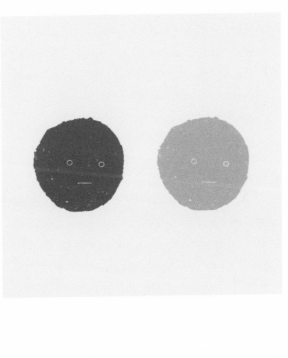

WHEN I GOT TO THE PLACE WHERE MY friends and I would meet up on our way to school, everyone else was already there. Both of the tengu followed behind me. Nobody said anything. It seemed as if the tengu were invisible. I wondered if my friends were just pretending not to notice.

I always walked at the back of the group. I couldn't seem to help lagging behind. Now that we were outside, the tengu were quiet. They followed very closely as we walked. Something about the way they followed me— so near and so silently—made it feel as though I were being rushed along. But because the tengu were there that day, I couldn't dawdle as much as I usually did, bringing up the rear.

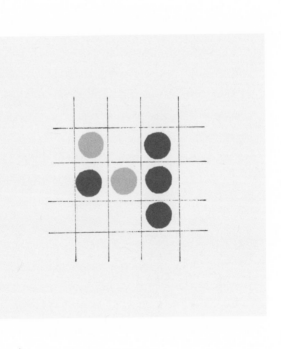

I WAS SURPRISED WHEN I GOT TO THE classroom. Beside Minami there was a badger; a little old lady was sitting next to Nishida; and I could have sworn that Oda was arm in arm with another creature from folklore, a *rokurokubi* woman with a very long neck. Before today, there had never been any sign of these creatures—I was sure of that.

I went over to Nishida and quietly ventured a question.

"What's with the old lady next to you? How long has she been there?"

"She's been here for a while," Nishida replied matter-of-factly.

"What?"

"Omachi, it's only because those people latched on to you that now you can see her too." As she said "those people," Nishida nodded her chin ever so slightly in the direction of the two tengu.

"She appeared by my side about a year ago. Oda's has been around since we started elementary school, and Minami says his has been with him since before he started kindergarten," Nishida said in a whisper. Even though no one else in the classroom seemed to be paying any attention to our conversation, we spoke to each other quite conspiratorially.

Nishida told me that the old lady who followed her around was known as a sand-throwing hag. I asked if it wasn't rude to call her a hag, and Nishida replied, "My dad said that's what they've always been called, so it's okay." Apparently Nishida's father could also see the sand-throwing hag. But, Nishida said, her mother could not.

"Cool, Omachi—you've got two critters," Minami called out as he passed by.

"They're not critters, they're people!" I corrected him.

"Oh. Sorry."

I was amazed not to be the only one who had something following me.

"Nishida, weren't you surprised when it happened to you?" I asked.

She thought about it for a moment.

"Only at first," she said. "I got used to her right away." That was probably true. The fact was, I myself was already growing accustomed to mine.

The tengu sat quietly on either side of me until third period, but after that they went off somewhere. The next thing I knew, the badger, the sand-throwing hag, and the rokurokubi woman with the long neck were also gone.

"They'll be back, once it gets dark," Oda whispered in my ear.

"They seem like they're pretty busy."

The aroma of our school lunch wafted in from the hallway. A burst of laughter erupted in another classroom. The row of poplar trees in the schoolyard caught the sunlight and glistened.

WHEN I HAPPENED TO LOOK OVER AT Sensei, his eyes were closed. The palm of his hand was still resting in mine. Sensei, I called to him, and he opened his eyes wide. "I'm awake," he replied in a low growl.

"Continue," Sensei prompted, sounding just like a schoolteacher.

AFTER A LITTLE WHILE, I BEGAN TO UN-
derstand some of what the tengu were saying.

"Because you spend a lot of time together,
you can relate more to one another," my
mother said. The one with the dark red face
was male, and the one with the pale red face
was female—that much I could tell.

"It was annoying that the boys skipped
out during cleaning time at school today," I
grumbled, and both of the tengu murmured
in assent with me. They made a bristling
sound, like "iga-iga-iga."

"What if I don't show Mom my bad grade
on the test?" When I conferred with the tengu
about this, the one with the dark red face
agreed with me—"gai-i-i"—but the one with
the pale red face shook her head—"i-ge-ge-ge."
I kept the test hidden at the back of my desk for

a while, but the one with the pale red face kept making such a fuss that eventually I ended up showing it to my mother.

"The tengu depend upon you, Tsuki, dear. You must take great care of your relationship with them," my mother said. Meanwhile, she wasn't all that angry about my test marks. I couldn't help but wonder what it all meant, though I didn't think too hard about it.

One time I had tried asking Nishida, "Why do you think these types have latched on to us?"

"I'm not really sure. But you know, there are plenty of other things out there that don't make sense, right?" I was impressed by the lack of concern in Nishida's response. She was right about that. The truth was, I myself wasn't all that interested in the reason. I had just felt like asking the question.

"Mom, were there tengu by your side when you were little?" This was another question I asked without really expecting anything to come of it.

"In my case, it was a fox instead of the tengu," my mother replied with a smile.

"How long has it been since it's been gone?"

"That's a secret."

I liked having the tengu around, but there were times when I felt depressed. It was fine when the two of them were chattering to each other, but when they sat still and just stared at me I wanted to tell them to get lost. Even if I didn't actually ever say that to them.

"HOW BIG WERE THE TENGU?" SENSEI asked.

"They must have been a little bigger than I was."

"This was around when you were in third grade, wasn't it, Tsukiko? If they were about your size, those were small tengu."

"I guess you're right. Now that you mention it, they must have been tengu kids."

Sensei turned to lie on his back with his hands folded behind his head. The palm of my hand felt lonesome, now that Sensei had taken his away. We continued our conversation across the low table as we looked up at the ceiling.

IT MUST HAVE BEEN DURING THE SECOND school term when the one with the pale red face seemed to fall ill. She looked thin, and even lost all interest in licking the margarine. She wasn't drinking any flower nectar either. Both of the tengu liked nectar. When the azaleas by the side of the road were in bloom, the tengu would cling to the base of the shrubs, slurping up the nectar from the flowers greedily. They wouldn't pluck a flower to taste the nectar, the way you and I might—they knew how to extract it deftly while leaving the blossoms intact on the branches.

DESPITE BEING SICK, THE ONE WITH THE pale red face still followed me to school. She would lie on the floor of the classroom, not moving, even if someone stepped on her. Most of the students didn't know she was there in the first place, so this was to be expected, but it still pained me whenever it happened.

It was probably after that whole thing started—that's when the tengu fell ill.

By "that whole thing," I mean when Yuko was ostracized.

At some point, a group of girls had decided to stop talking to her. Before long, a few of the boys went along with it too. The more ordinary students—like Nishida and me—we pretended not to notice what they were doing.

EVEN AS THE SHUNNING GOT WORSE AND worse, Yuko never once cried. During class, she would look straight at the teacher, and raise her hand often. Whenever Yuko answered a question, half of the students in class would coldly turn their heads away. Sometimes one of the girls even murmured, "Jerk," under her breath. Her voice sounded terribly nasty. Whenever I imagined someone speaking to me in that tone, it made shivers run up and down my spine.

During recess, Yuko was always reading a book. Nishida's sand-throwing hag hadn't been feeling well either. Still, she wasn't in as bad shape as my pale red tengu. Meanwhile, the badger and the rokurokubi woman with the very long neck would wander around the room during class. Everyone seemed restless.

Yuko and I went to the same abacus school after regular school. It was one station away by train, so Yuko and I were the only ones from our class who went there. At the abacus school, Yuko chatted with all the other students. She laughed and smiled too—she wasn't always just reading a book. One time, she even did an impersonation of the comedian Hitoshi Ueki and his catchphrase, "Look at that—I did it again!" She didn't really sound much like him, though.

THE TENGU WITH THE PALE RED FACE wasn't well when we were at abacus school either. In class, I would sit in a corner, trying to avoid making eye contact with Yuko. As for Yuko, there were several times when it seemed like she might have wanted to say something to me, but I guess I was unconsciously avoiding her. I didn't know what to do. And, for some reason, I was scared.

ON THE TRAIN HOME, YUKO WOULD ALWAYS stand in the same spot by the door, and I normally boarded from a different place on the platform. But one day I had jumped onto the train just before it left the station, and practically bumped into Yuko. I hadn't noticed that she was right there. Yuko uttered a small sound of surprise. I kept my eyes lowered. We rode in awkward silence until we got off at our stop.

I kept my head down even while we walked beside each other from the station. I was panicking about what would happen if one of the girls from our class saw me walking with Yuko. My heart was really pounding in my chest—it was terrible. I felt like cringing, all the way down to the tips of my fingers.

"You don't have to walk next to me,

Omachi," Yuko murmured after a while. "What?" I replied idiotically. I can still remember the tremendous relief I felt then. In that same instant of relief, I was overcome with intense self-loathing. But really I was relieved.

When I looked up at Yuko, she was smiling. And yet her smiling face reminded me of the face of my grandmother, who had died the year before, and what she had looked like when she was laid out in her coffin.

I REALIZED SOMETHING IN THAT MOMENT. Yuko had somehow resigned herself to the situation. She had given up being sad or being disappointed. Just like my grandmother when she had taken her last breath, Yuko had purposely stopped feeling things.

Was it even possible to do that? I wondered. But the expression on Yuko's face right before my eyes seemed to suggest that it most certainly was.

"What's the matter, Omachi?" Yuko asked. I was staring straight at her. Our eyes met. Before I knew it, I was telling her about the tengu.

"WHAT KIND OF VOICE DID THIS YUKO have?" Sensei asked.

I couldn't recall much about what Yuko sounded like. I think she may have had a soft voice. I remembered that the tengu had loud voices, but when I tried to summon other details, I couldn't really remember what the tengu sounded like either.

I may have said that I started telling Yuko about the tengu, but I didn't really go into detail. Though when I mentioned that the one with the pale red face had been sick ever since this stuff with her had been going on, Yuko seemed startled. Then she let out several deep sighs.

"I appreciate that, even if it's from the tengu," Yuko murmured, as her breathing grew regular again.

I didn't know how to respond. Up until then, all I had done was pretend not to notice. I couldn't honestly reply with something like "I know, right?" Of course, I told little white lies every so often, but I was aware that now was definitely not a time for dishonesty. And I didn't mean "definitely" in a generic, conversational way—this was absolutely definitely not the time.

We walked along in silence. When we were about to part ways, I said, "The tengu—they're still here behind me." Yuko waved to them and said, in English, "Goodbye." Her wave was slightly in the wrong direction, but both of the tengu still waved back at her.

AROUND THE TIME OF THE SECOND-TERM closing ceremony—as we were preparing to head into the third term—the girls seemed to forget about ostracizing Yuko. After that, they did a bit of the same to Nishida, but it didn't really amount to much. This kind of thing tended to ebb and flow. It was a cruel game, administered according to sheer whim.

There were still plenty of times when Yuko was alone, but the others seemed to pretend that what had been going on during the previous term had never happened. From time to time I would notice Yuko sitting quietly in a corner of the classroom, either reading a book or daydreaming. I hardly ever spoke to her at school. It wasn't as if we had been friends with each other in the first place.

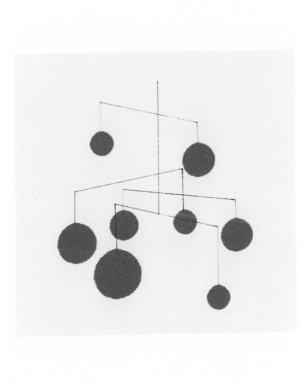

OCCASIONALLY, I'D SEE YUKO TALKING TO another girl. Even when I could hear the other girl's voice, I couldn't hear Yuko's at all. Although she was right there, it seemed as if she wasn't. I couldn't be sure whether she actually existed.

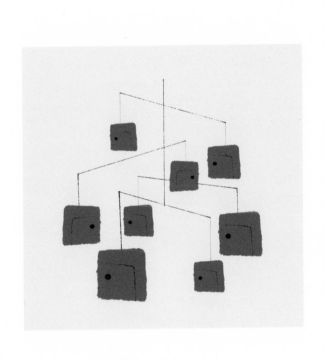

ONCE A DAY, EVERY DAY, BOTH OF the tengu would go over to Yuko and touch her. When they did so, the spot on Yuko's body where they had touched her would sparkle. Like a nighttime parade. Those flashes of light were pretty, but there was something terribly sad about them too.

THE ONE WITH THE PALE RED FACE RE-
covered from her illness. She was no longer
lying down in the classroom either. I had
grown three centimeters taller—I was now
about the same height as both of the tengu.
I had the feeling that time was passing by so
quickly, faster than it had last year. When I told
my mother this, she laughed off my concern.
"For me, a year goes by in the blink of an eye!"

Every so often, Yuko and I ended up together on the way home from abacus school.
Whenever we parted ways, Yuko would always direct a "goodbye" to the space behind
me. She did it even when neither of the tengu
were there, but I didn't tell her that.

There was something very kind about
Yuko's "goodbye." I wondered if my voice
would ever sound as kind as that. If it did,

would the tengu touch me, and would the spot where they touched sparkle? And if my voice ever did sound like that, would the tengu still be following me? This is what I always thought about while I watched Yuko's retreating figure disappear around a corner.

"SO DOES YOUR VOICE EVER SOUND LIKE that, Tsukiko?" Sensei asked. He was still lying there, faceup.

"Not at all. Wouldn't you agree?"

"Not at all, that's for sure."

"That's a rude thing to say."

Sensei and I gazed up at the ceiling for a while. The grain of the wood resembled various animals. A dog. A snake. A tiger. A squirrel.

"Ah, look, there's a tengu." Sensei said, pointing at the ceiling. I stared at the spot where Sensei had pointed, and indeed, a pattern in the shape of a tengu began to emerge.

"How long did the tengu stay?" Sensei asked quietly.

"That's a secret."

I see, Sensei murmured with a laugh. The buzzing of the cicadas had grown louder again. The breeze swept in, carrying the evening air with it. Stories from long ago are quite good, aren't they? Sensei said. I'm the one who told the story, I boasted. But I was the one who asked you to tell the story. Sensei laughed again. The warmth I had felt on Sensei's palm swelled all around him—I could sense it even without touching him. *Sensei would just always be so . . . Sensei.* I laughed too, as I stared up at the tengu on the ceiling. In the distance, the evening cicadas had begun to sing.

AFTERWORD

Sometimes I think about stories that have ended.

As the author of these stories, I have created so many different episodes and emotions. In the moment, when I am writing them down, these people and events become just as real to me as anything else that exists in the world.

However, once I have finished writing, all those real things that "existed" for me become part of the past—a memory—just like what happens to things in the present, within everyday real life.

As time goes by, I find myself thinking again about a certain story. I wonder, *Is that world really over and done with?*

Take the story of *Strange Weather in Tokyo.*

What happened to Tsukiko after Sensei died? What about Takashi Kojima? And Satoru's bar? And if I were to go even further back, to when Sensei was still alive, I wonder how Tsukiko and Sensei really spent their time, day by day. When they weren't meeting up at the bar. When they were on their own. Or on their occasional dates. Did they go on any more trips together?

These are some of the thoughts that have passed through my mind since I finished writing that book. All the things that I wasn't able to include in that book—things that even I, as the author, don't know about Sensei and Tsukiko's time together. Like echoes that I hear, far off in the distance.

This book might describe a day that Tsukiko and Sensei spent together in early summer. On another day, presumably they passed their time differently.

The world that exists behind a story is never fully known, not even to the author. That is what I had in mind as I created this. I hope you have enjoyed reading this memento of a story that has ended.

HIROMI KAWAKAMI was born in Tokyo in 1958. Her first book, *God (Kamisama)*, was published in 1994. In 1996, she was awarded the Akutagawa Prize for *Tread on a Snake (Hebi o fumu)*, and in 2001 she won the Tanizaki Prize for her novel *Strange Weather in Tokyo (Sensei no kaban)*, which was an international bestseller. The book was short-listed for the 2012 Man Asian Literary Prize and the 2014 International Foreign Fiction Prize.

ALLISON MARKIN POWELL is a translator, editor, and publishing consultant. In addition to Hiromi Kawakami's *Strange Weather in Tokyo*, *The Nakano Thrift Shop*, and *The Ten Loves of Nishino*, she has translated books by Osamu Dazai and Fuminori Nakamura, and her work has appeared in *Words Without Borders* and *Granta*, among other publications. She maintains the database japaneseliteratureinenglish.com.